THE WIS

A CARAVAN OF CARTS LED BY AN ELDERLY MERCHANT WAS ABOUT TO ENTER A DESERT.

THE THOUGHT OF CROSSING THAT DESERT FRIGHTENS ME.
I'D BE HAPPIER IF WE HAD A BOLDER MAN TO LEAD US. OUR OLD MASTER IS MUCH TOO CAUTIOUS FOR MY LIKING.
I AGREE WITH YOU.

WE SHOULD HAVE BEEN IN THE CARAVAN OF THAT SMART YOUNG MERCHANT WHO VISITED OUR CAMP SOME DAYS AGO.

YES, WE SHOULD HAVE. HOW CLEVERLY HE TALKED OUR MASTER INTO LETTING HIM GO AHEAD OF US! HE MUST BE OUT OF THE DESERT BY NOW, THE LUCKY MAN!

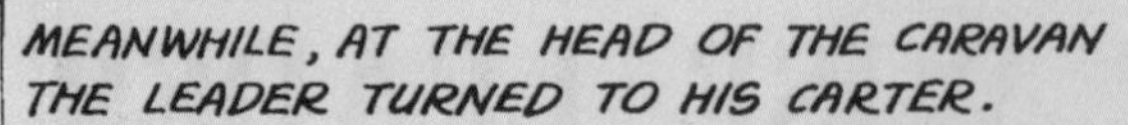
MEANWHILE, AT THE HEAD OF THE CARAVAN THE LEADER TURNED TO HIS CARTER.

DO WE HAVE ENOUGH WATER?
YES, SIR. ALL OUR JARS ARE FULL...

...THANKS TO THOSE FRESHLY DUG WELLS WE FOUND ALL ALONG THE WAY. I WONDER WHO DUG THEM?

WHO ELSE BUT THAT YOUNG MERCHANT WHO CAME TO SEE ME IN THE CITY. NOW YOU KNOW WHY I AGREED TO LET HIS CARAVAN GO AHEAD OF OURS.

DIGGING WELLS IS HARD WORK. I DID NOT WANT TO LEAD EXHAUSTED MEN ACROSS THIS ARID DESERT.

FROM NOW ON WE MUST CONSERVE EVERY DROP OF WATER WE HAVE. IT'LL TAKE US SEVERAL DAYS TO CROSS THIS BARREN, SUN-SCORCHED DESERT. AND YOU CAN BE SURE WE WON'T FIND ANY WATER ALONG THE WAY.

THE CARAVAN ENTERED THE DESERT AND BEGAN TO MAKE SLOW, BUT STEADY PROGRESS. SEVERAL MILES LATER —
THOSE PEOPLE SEEM TO BE HEADING THIS WAY.

I WONDER WHO THEY ARE.

GREETINGS TO YOU, SIR. YOU MUST HAVE COME FROM VARANASI.

YOUR MEN LOOK TIRED. THEY COULD REFRESH THEMSELVES WHEN YOU REACH THE FOREST.
WHICH FOREST ARE YOU TALKING ABOUT?

THE GREAT FOREST BEYOND THOSE SAND DUNES.

IT'S FULL OF LAKES AND POOLS. THAT'S WHERE WE FOUND THESE LOTUSES AND WATER-LILIES.

YOU MUST HAVE NOTICED THAT OUR CLOTHES ARE DRENCHED. IT WAS RAINING HEAVILY THERE JUST NOW.

HMMM...

LOOK AT THE AMOUNT OF WATER THEY ARE CARRYING, CHIEF.
SHEER MADNESS!

THOSE HEAVILY-LADEN CARTS WILL ONLY SLOW DOWN YOUR PROGRESS, SIR. EMPTY THOSE JARS. YOU WON'T NEED THE WATER.

THANK YOU FOR THE ADVICE, FRIEND. BUT I PREFER TO KEEP THE WATER.
KEEP IT BY ALL MEANS!

BUT IF I WERE YOU I'D GET RID OF THAT BURDEN. FOR THE SOONER YOU GET OUT OF THIS DESERT, THE BETTER FOR ALL OF YOU.

FAREWELL!

THOSE PEOPLE ARE RIGHT. WE ARE CRAWLING AT A SNAIL'S PACE BECAUSE OF THOSE WATER-JARS.
LET'S DO AS THEY ADVISED.

IF THERE ARE LAKES AHEAD WHY SHOULD WE CARRY ALL THAT WATER?
I'LL TELL YOU WHY.

THOSE PEOPLE WERE MAN-EATING DEMONS. THEY WERE TRYING TO TRICK US INTO THROWING AWAY OUR WATER.

THEY KNOW WE ARE TOO STRONG FOR THEM NOW. BUT WITHOUT WATER WE WOULD SOON LOSE OUR STRENGTH AND FALL PREY TO THEM.

YOU CAN BE SURE THERE ARE NO FORESTS OR POOLS AHEAD. GET BACK INTO THE CARTS AND LET'S MOVE ON.

THE CARAVAN RESUMED ITS JOURNEY.

MAN-EATING DEMONS! HA! NEXT HE'LL START IMAGINING THAT OUR BULLOCKS ARE DEMONS.
HOW I WISH WE HAD JOINED THAT YOUNG MERCHANT'S CARAVAN!

YOU'RE TELLING ME! HE HAS BRAINS, THAT MAN. HE WOULDN'T GO ABOUT SEEING DEMONS IN INNOCENT TRAVELLERS.

WE'LL TALK TO THE OTHERS AGAIN ABOUT... HEY, WHAT'S THAT...!

IT'S SOME SORT OF WRECKAGE.

GOOD GOD! THE REMAINS OF A CARAVAN!
I... I...

I HAVE A FEELING IT'S THE CARAVAN OF THAT YOUNG MERCHANT WE WERE SO EAGER TO JOIN!

SIR, IS THAT THE CARAVAN WHICH WENT AHEAD OF US?
I'M AFRAID SO.

THE DEMONS MUST HAVE TRICKED THEM IN THE SAME WAY AS THEY TRIED TO TRICK US.

THEY HAVE DEVOURED THE MEN. LOOK AT THE BONES LYING ALL AROUND.

I...I'M ASHAMED OF MYSELF, SIR.
SO AM I, SIR. BUT I...I STILL CAN'T BELIEVE THEY WERE REAL DEMONS!

I DON'T BLAME YOU. THOSE DEMONS COULD HAVE FOOLED ANYONE.
HOW DID YOU KNOW THEY WERE LYING, SIR?

THEY SAID IT WAS RAINING HEAVILY IN THE FOREST WHICH ACCORDING TO THEM WAS NOT TOO FAR AWAY.

BUT WHEN I LOOKED UP, I COULD NOT SEE A RAIN CLOUD ANYWHERE IN THE SKY.

THAT MADE ME SUSPICIOUS. THEN I LOOKED CLOSELY AT THEM AND SAW THAT THEIR EYES WERE ROUND AND RED LIKE THOSE OF DEMONS.

THEN I KNEW THEY WERE NOT ORDINARY MEN.

I AM SURE THEY ARE STILL WATCHING US FROM THE TOP OF THOSE DUNES.

ON THE DUNES —
THEY ARE LOOKING THIS WAY.
OUR TRICK HAS FAILED. I WAS HOPING HIS MEN WOULD REBEL AND THROW OUT THE WATER.

BUT THERE'S NO CHANCE OF THAT HAPPENING NOW. LET'S GO BACK.

AS THE CARTERS DROVE ON —
YOU KNOW, WE ARE LUCKY WE CHOSE TO WORK FOR SUCH A WISE LEADER.
YOU'RE TELLING ME! HE HAS BRAINS, THAT MAN!

THE PRINCE AND THE SEEDLING

A CERTAIN KING WAS WORRIED ABOUT HIS SON.

HE IS SO WILFUL AND UNRULY. THE MINISTERS FEAR HIM, THE PEOPLE FEAR HIM... EVEN I FEAR HIM! WHAT AM I TO DO?

THEN ONE DAY HE APPROACHED A GREAT SAGE.
ONLY YOU CAN REFORM MY SON, HOLY SIR.
SEND HIM TO ME.

WHEN THE PRINCE CAME, THE SAGE TOOK HIM TO A CORNER OF THE GARDEN AND SHOWED HIM A NEEM SEEDLING.
PLUCK ONE OF THOSE LEAVES AND TASTE IT.

THE PRINCE PLUCKED A LEAF.

BUT THE MOMENT HE PUT IT INTO HIS MOUTH—

UGH! WHAT A BITTER TASTE!

IF THE YOUNG PLANT CAN BE SO BITTER, I CAN'T IMAGINE WHAT THE FULL-GROWN TREE WILL BE LIKE.

I WON'T LET IT GROW!

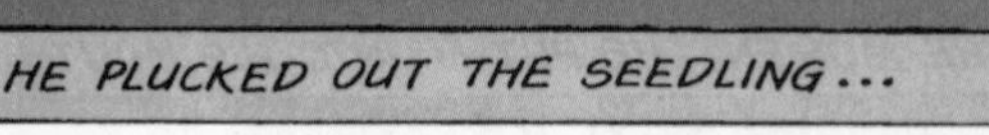
HE PLUCKED OUT THE SEEDLING...

...AND TORE IT TO PIECES.

SO TOO WILL THE PEOPLE DESTROY YOU, SON. FOR...

...IF YOU AS A MERE PRINCE CAN BE SO FIERCE, WHAT WILL YOU BE LIKE WHEN YOU ARE A KING?
YOU HAVE OPENED MY EYES, HOLY SIR. I WILL MEND MY WAYS.

THE PRINCE KEPT HIS PROMISE AND HE BECAME GENTLE AND KIND. AND YEARS LATER WHEN HIS FATHER DIED, THE PEOPLE HAD NO HESITATION IN MAKING HIM KING.

THE CLEVER SON

ONE MORNING A MAN COAXED HIS AGED FATHER TO GO OUT WITH HIM.

WHERE ARE YOU TAKING GRANDFATHER?
INTO TOWN.

THEN I'M COMING TOO.
NO, SON. YOU STAY HERE. YOUR MOTHER WILL GIVE YOU SWEETS.

COME INSIDE. I'LL SHOW YOU THE SWEETMEATS FATHER BROUGHT FOR YOU YESTERDAY.

COME BACK!

BUT THE BOY RAN AFTER THE CART AND JUMPED INTO IT.
I WANT TO COME WITH YOU, GRANDFATHER!
WHAT A NUISANCE HE IS! I'LL HAVE TO TAKE HIM ALONG NOW.

BUT I'LL MAKE SURE HE DOES NOT SEE ANYTHING.

THE MAN STOPPED THE CART OUTSIDE A GRAVEYARD.
YOU TWO WAIT HERE. I'LL BE BACK SOON.

THEN GOING TO A SECLUDED SPOT IN THE GRAVEYARD HE BEGAN TO DIG.

AFTER A WHILE, HIS SON CAME IN SEARCH OF HIM.

FATHER!

WHAT ARE YOU DOING HERE ? GO BACK TO YOUR GRANDFATHER!

WHAT ARE YOU DOING FATHER ?
I AM DIGGING! CAN'T YOU SEE ?

WHY, FATHER ? IS THERE SOMETHING HIDDEN THERE ?
I'D BETTER TELL HIM THE TRUTH.

SON, I AM DIGGING A GRAVE ...

... FOR YOUR GRANDFATHER.
FOR GRANDFATHER?

BUT HE'S NOT DEAD! HE'S STILL ALIVE!

YES! YES! BUT HE HAS BECOME TOO OLD. HE IS USELESS. HE DOES NO WORK AROUND THE HOUSE AND HE EATS TOO MUCH.

HE DOESN'T HAVE LONG TO LIVE ANYWAY, SO...

...YOUR MOTHER AND I FELT THERE WAS NO HARM IN BURYING HIM RIGHT AWAY.
OH!

I'M GLAD YOU TOLD ME ALL THIS, FATHER.
I KNOW I CAN TRUST YOU WITH A SECRET.

NOW MAY I HAVE THE SPADE FOR A WHILE?
?

WHAT IS HE UP TO? WHERE IS HE TAKING THE SPADE?

THE MAN FOLLOWED THE BOY.
WHAT ARE YOU DOING, SON?
DIGGING, FATHER.

WHAT ARE YOU TALKING ABOUT?
I DON'T WANT TO MAKE YOU WAIT.

WHEN YOU BECOME OLD, I DON'T WANT TO MAKE YOU WAIT OUTSIDE TILL I DIG YOUR GRAVE.

I'LL BRING YOU STRAIGHT HERE AND PUSH YOU INTO THIS PIT.
WHAT! YOU WOULD BURY ME ALIVE!

HOW COULD YOU THINK OF DOING SUCH A THING TO ME, YOUR FATHER!
BUT FATHER THAT'S WHAT YOU ARE ABOUT TO DO TO YOUR FATHER!

I WOULD LIKE TO HONOUR THE FAMILY TRADITION.

OH, GOD! I WAS ABOUT TO SET SUCH A WICKED EXAMPLE!

SON, YOU HAVE OPENED MY EYES.

YOU HAVE SAVED ME FROM COMMITTING A TERRIBLE SIN!

COME, LET US TAKE GRANDFATHER HOME.
THE MAN TOOK HIS FATHER BACK AND LOVINGLY CARED FOR HIM FOR THE REST OF HIS LIFE.

THE FRUIT TREE

THE ONLY WORK THE MEN OF A CERTAIN VILLAGE DID WAS TO WATCH OVER A TREE GROWING BY THE ROADSIDE.

ANY LUCK SO FAR ?
SSS-SH! THERE'S A MAN EATING THE FRUIT.

LOOKS RICH ENOUGH ... A GOOD START TO THE DAY, WHAT ?

HE'S GOING AWAY. FOLLOW HIM.

OOOOH !
THE POISON IS TAKING EFFECT.

HE'S DEAD. COME ON. LET'S GET TO WORK.
THUMP

THAT TREE WILL MAKE US ALL RICH.
YES! EVERYBODY WHO COMES BY, MISTAKES THOSE POISONOUS FRUIT FOR MANGOES... HEEHEEHEE!

THAT TREE IS OUR KALPAVRIKSHA*!

THEN ONE DAY —
I SAW FOUR MEN COMING THIS WAY. KEEP OUT OF SIGHT.

THE FOUR MEN WERE PART OF A CARAVAN COMING BEHIND THEM.
LOOK, MANGOES!

I'LL GO UP AND THROW SOME DOWN.

* WISH-TREE

THE MEN COLLECTED A SMALL PILE OF THE FRUIT.

BUT JUST AS THEY BEGAN TO EAT IT, THE REST OF THE CARAVAN CAME UP. WHEN THE MERCHANT, WHO WAS LEADING THE CARAVAN, SAW WHAT HIS MEN WERE DOING —
STOP! DON'T EAT THAT FRUIT!

IT'S POISONOUS!
POISONOUS! ...I'VE ALREADY EATEN ONE!
SO HAVE I!

THE MERCHANT GAVE THEM AN ANTIDOTE.
DRINK THIS AT ONCE!

IT'LL MAKE YOU VOMIT THE POISON.

WHAT'S HAPPENING! HOW DID HE KNOW THE FRUIT WERE POISONOUS?
THAT'S WHAT I'D LIKE TO KNOW.

THERE MUST BE SOME MARK ON THAT TREE.
THEN WE HAD BETTER FIND OUT WHAT IT IS AND REMOVE IT.

IT WOULD BE BAD FOR BUSINESS IF OTHER TRAVELLERS TOO KEPT AWAY FROM THAT TREE.

THE VILLAGERS CAME OUT OF THEIR HIDING-PLACE.
HEAVEN HELP US! WHAT'S GOING ON HERE!

GOOD SIR, I HOPE YOUR MEN HAVE NOT EATEN ANY OF THAT FRUIT.
NO. THEY HAVEN'T.

I CAME ON THE SCENE JUST IN TIME.
MANY TRAVELLERS WHO PASS BY, MISTAKE THEM FOR MANGOES.

HOW DID YOU KNOW THEY WERE NOT MANGOES BUT POISONOUS FRUIT?
IT WASN'T DIFFICULT.

A TREE GROWING NEAR A VILLAGE IS SOON DEPRIVED OF ITS FRUIT BY THE VILLAGERS AND THEIR CHILDREN.

BUT THIS TREE, THOUGH EASY TO CLIMB AND LADEN WITH FRUIT, HAS BEEN LEFT UNTOUCHED BY THE PEOPLE OF YOUR VILLAGE.

HENCE I CONCLUDED THAT ITS FRUITS WERE POISONOUS.

NOW BEFORE WE GO WE'LL CUT DOWN THE TREE.
WHAT! I MEAN... YES, THAT'S THE BEST THING TO DO.

A LITTLE LATER THE CARAVAN RESUMED ITS JOURNEY LEAVING SOME VERY DISAPPOINTED MEN BEHIND.

THE TWO KINGS
A POWERFUL AND JUST KING NAMED MALLIKA ONCE RULED OVER THE KINGDOM OF KOSALA.

GREAT THOUGH HIS ACHIEVEMENTS WERE, HE WAS PLAGUED BY SELF-DOUBT.
AM I REALLY AS GOOD AS PEOPLE SAY I AM?

HE QUESTIONED HIS MINISTER.
TELL ME THE TRUTH. IS THERE ANY FLAW IN MY CHARACTER?
NO, YOUR MAJESTY.

YOU ARE GENTLE, GENEROUS AND JUST.

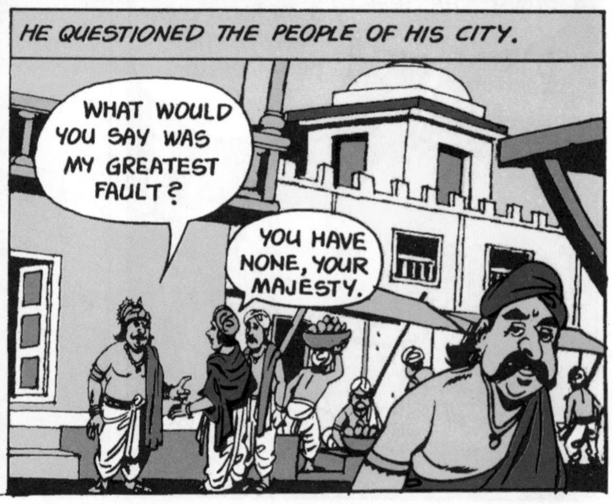
HE QUESTIONED THE PEOPLE OF HIS CITY.
WHAT WOULD YOU SAY WAS MY GREATEST FAULT?
YOU HAVE NONE, YOUR MAJESTY.

YOU RULE US WISELY AND WELL.
YES, INDEED, YOU DO.

PERHAPS MY MINISTERS AND MY PEOPLE ARE AFRAID TO SPEAK OUT. I'LL GO TO THE COUNTRYSIDE WHERE THEY DO NOT KNOW ME.

SO HE GOT INTO A CHARIOT AND SET OUT.

HIS CHARIOTEER DROVE HIM WHEREVER HE WISHED TO GO ...

...BUT NOWHERE COULD HE FIND A MAN WHO COULD, OR WOULD, POINT OUT HIS FAULTS TO HIM.
... THERE IS NO ONE AS VIRTUOUS AS OUR GREAT KING, MALLIKA.

THEN ONE DAY AS HIS CHARIOT WAS ABOUT TO CROSS A NARROW BRIDGE —
HO, THERE! HOLD BACK YOUR HORSES.

LET NO ONE COME IN THE WAY OF MY ROYAL MASTER, BRAHMADATTA, KING OF VARANASI.

WELL, MY MASTER IS THE LORD OF KOSALA. I CANNOT MOVE ASIDE FOR ANYONE.
IT WAS THE PRACTICE IN THOSE DAYS THAT THE MAN OF LOWER STATUS SHOULD GIVE THE RIGHT OF WAY TO HIS SUPERIOR.

BOTH OF US ARE CARRYING ROYAL PERSONAGES. NOW WHO SHOULD MOVE ASIDE FOR WHOM?
LET AGE OR POWER DECIDE THAT. HOW OLD IS YOUR MASTER? HOW LARGE IS HIS KINGDOM?

BUT IT SO HAPPENED THAT BOTH THE KINGS WERE OF THE SAME AGE AND BOTH THEIR KINGDOMS WERE OF THE SAME SIZE.
NOW WHAT ARE WE TO DO?
LET THE BETTER MAN HAVE THE RIGHT OF WAY.

WHO IS THE BETTER MAN? WHAT ARE YOUR MASTER'S VIRTUES?
MY MASTER REPAYS EVIL FOR EVIL AND GOOD FOR GOOD.

IF THOSE ARE YOUR MASTER'S VIRTUES I SHUDDER TO THINK WHAT HIS FAULTS ARE.
AT LAST I HAVE MET SOMEONE WHO IS NOT AFRAID TO SPEAK HIS MIND.

ENOUGH OF YOUR INSOLENCE! LET'S HEAR WHAT YOUR OWN MASTER'S VIRTUES ARE.
THAT IS SOMETHING I WOULD LIKE TO HEAR TOO.

MY MASTER REPAYS GOOD FOR EVIL. HE DOES GOOD EVEN TO THOSE WHO DO HIM HARM.

THEN HE IS A BETTER MAN THAN I.

I SALUTE YOU, O KING.

NOW I KNOW WHAT MY FAULTS ARE AND HOW FAR SHORT OF THE MARK I FALL. COME, LET'S DRAW BACK OUR CHARIOT AND LET KING BRAHMADATTA PASS.

OUSHADHAKUMARA

OUSHADHAKUMARA WAS A GREAT SAGE. HE BECAME FAMOUS FOR HIS WISDOM WHEN HE WAS STILL VERY YOUNG.

ONCE, TWO WOMEN, BOTH CLAIMING TO BE THE MOTHER OF THE SAME CHILD, CAME TO HIM FOR ARBITRATION.

THIS CHILD IS MINE.
NO, HE IS MINE. SHE STOLE HIM FROM ME.

OUSHADHAKUMARA DREW A LINE ON THE GROUND AND PLACED THE CHILD ON IT.

NOW STAND ON EITHER SIDE OF THE LINE AND TAKE HOLD OF THE CHILD.

THE ONE WHO CAN PULL THE CHILD OVER THE LINE TO HER SIDE CAN KEEP IT.

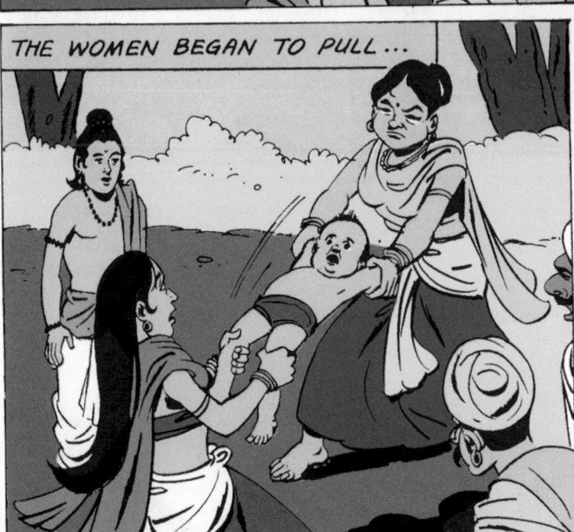
THE WOMEN BEGAN TO PULL ...

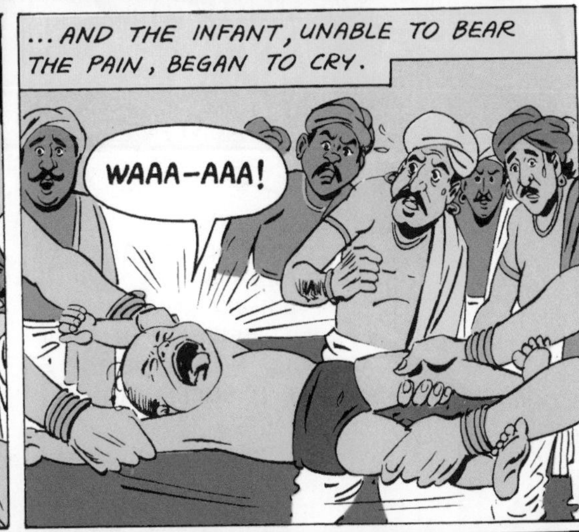
... AND THE INFANT, UNABLE TO BEAR THE PAIN, BEGAN TO CRY.
WAAA-AAA!

THEN ONE OF THE WOMEN IMMEDI-ATELY LET GO HER GRIP ON THE CHILD ...

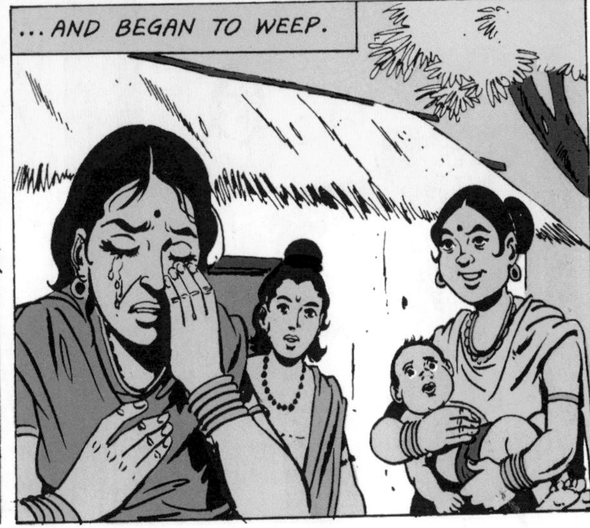
... AND BEGAN TO WEEP.

THE CHILD IS MINE!

NOT SO! THE CHILD IS HERS. GIVE IT TO HER.
WHAT DO YOU MEAN? DIDN'T I PULL IT OVER THE LINE? I'VE WON. THE CHILD BELONGS TO ME.

NO. THE CHILD BELONGS TO HER. SHE LET GO HER HOLD ON THE CHILD BECAUSE SHE COULD NOT BEAR TO SEE IT SUFFERING.

BUT YOU HAD NO MERCY. HOW COULD YOU BE THE MOTHER OF THE CHILD?

ALL THE PEOPLE WERE AMAZED AT OUSHADHAKUMARA'S WISDOM AND HIS FAME SPREAD FAR AND WIDE.

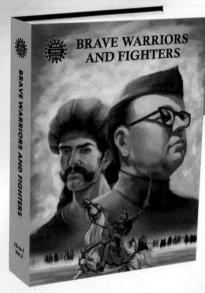